NIGHT NOISES

WRITTEN BY
Mem Fox

ILLUSTRATED BY
Terry Denton

Gulliver Books
Harcourt Brace Jovanovich, Publishers
San Diego   New York   London

Lily Laceby lived in an old cottage in the hills.

Her hair was as wispy
as cobwebs in ceilings.

Her bones were as creaky
as floorboards at midnight.

Her only companion was a fat old dog called Butch Aggie.
People who lived nearby said Lily was nearly ninety,
but they were only guessing.

One wild
winter's evening,

as Lily Laceby sat by her fire,
snug and warm, she drifted off to sleep
and began to dream.

Butch Aggie
dozed at her feet.

Outside, clouds raced along the sky,
playing hide-and-seek with the moon.
Wind and rain rattled at the windows,
and trees banged against the roof.

CLICK.
CLACK.

Somewhere
in the distance
car doors opened
and closed softly.

Butch Aggie listened . . .

but Lily Laceby
kept on dreaming.

CRINCH, CRUNCH.

Feet tiptoed
up the garden path.

Butch Aggie cocked her head . . .

but Lily Laceby
went on dreaming.

MURMUR, MUTTER, SHHHH.

Voices whispered
in bushes.

Butch Aggie bristled . . .

but Lily Laceby
went on dreaming.

SQUINT, PEEK, PEER.

Eyes peeped
through keyholes.

Butch Aggie's throat rumbled . . .

but Lily Laceby
went on dreaming.

TWIST, TEST, RATTLE.

Hands tried
to turn doorknobs.

Butch Aggie bared her teeth . . .

but Lily Laceby
went on dreaming.

KNICK, KNACK, KNOCK.

Knuckles drummed
on doorframes.

Butch Aggie leaped up, growling . . .

but Lily Laceby
went on dreaming.

Fists beat upon doors
and voices shouted at windows.

YELL,
CLATTER,
BANG,
BANG,
BANG,
BANG.

Butch Aggie barked and barked.

Lily Laceby
woke up
with a start.

"Who is it?" she called.
"Who is it on a night like this?"

"It's only us!"
"Let us in!"
"Let us in!"

CREAK, CRACK

went Lily Laceby's knees
as she got to her feet.

SNICK, SNACK

went the bolts on the door.

And in came . . .

her two sons . . .
her three daughters . . .
her fourteen grandchildren . . .
her thirty-five great-grandchildren . . .

her great-great-grandchild, Emily, aged four-and-a-half . . .
and her forty-seven friends.

"Are you really ninety?"
whispered Emily, aged four-and-a-half.

Lily Laceby held her hand and smiled.
"Inside I'm only four-and-a-half, like you," she whispered back.
"But don't tell anyone."

This book was written for Nana, Lily's daughter.

M. F.

For Dorothy and her game leg

T. D.

First published 1989 by Omnibus Books in association with Penguin Books Australia

Text copyright © 1989 by Mem Fox

Illustrations copyright © 1989 by Terry Denton

Requests for permission to make copies of any part
of the work should be mailed to:

Copyrights and Permissions Department,

Harcourt Brace Jovanovich, Publishers,

Orlando, Florida 32887.

Library of Congress Cataloging-in-Publication Data

Fox, Mem, 1946–

Night noises/written by Mem Fox; illustrated by Terry Denton.

p.   cm.

Summary: Old Lily Laceby dozes by the fire with her faithful dog
at her feet as strange night noises herald a surprising awakening.

ISBN 0-15-200543-9

[1. Night—Fiction.   2. Sleep—Fiction.]   I. Denton, Terry, ill.

II. Title

PZ7.F8393N1   1989

[E]—dc19   89-2162

Printed in Singapore

First United States Edition   A B C D E